Presenting... Tallulah

To Liam and Stella . . . I love you both for every inch of your beings inside and out, always and forever! Mommy xoxo —T. S.

For Zoe Samantha Newton and the family. Love, Mommy and Nester —V. B. N.

ALADDIN

An imprint of Simon & Schuster Children's Publishing Division

1230 Avenue of the Americas, New York, NY 10020

First Aladdin hardcover edition September 2010

Text copyright © 2010 by Tori Spelling

Illustrations copyright © 2010 by Vanessa Brantley Newton

All rights reserved, including the right of reproduction in whole or in part in any form.

ALADDIN is a trademark of Simon & Schuster, Inc., and related logo is a registered trademark of Simon & Schuster, Inc.

For information about special discounts for bulk purchases,

please contact Simon & Schuster Special Sales at 1-866-506-1949 or business@simonandschuster.com.

The Simon & Schuster Speakers Bureau can bring authors to your live event.

For more information or to book an event contact the Simon & Schuster Speakers Bureau

at 1-866-248-3049 or visit our website at www.simonspeakers.com.

Designed by Karin Paprocki

The text of this book was set in Elegante.

Manufactured in China

0610 SCP

2 4 6 8 10 9 7 5 3 1

Library of Congress Cataloging-in-Publication Data

Spelling, Tori, 1973–

Presenting . . . Tallulah / by Tori Spelling with Hilary Liftin ; illustrated by Vanessa Brantley Newton. — 1st Aladdin hardcover ed.

p. cm.

Summary: Tallulah is always being told what she cannot do because of the kind of girl people perceive her to be,

but with the help of the new boy in school, she finds a way to just be herself.

ISBN 978-1-4169-9404-6 (hardcover)

[1. Friendship—Fiction. 2. Self-acceptance—Fiction. 3. Individuality—Fiction.] I. Liftin, Hilary. II. Newton, Vanessa Brantley, ill. III. Title.

PZ7.S747243Pr 2010

[E]—dc22

2009033947

Presenting... Tallulah

By Tori Spelling
NEW YORK TIMES
BESTSELLING AUTHOR

Illustrated by
VANESSA BRANTLEY NEWTON

Aladdin
NEW YORK LONDON TORONTO SYDNEY

T ALLULAH was not
supposed to get dirty.

Or talk loudly.

Or make

a mess.

"You're not

that kind of girl,"

everybody said.

Tallulah was not allowed to wear jeans to school.

Or keep her hair down the way she wanted.

Or wear the sneakers that all

the other kids wore.

"You're not like all the other kids," said her mother.

Tallulah was not allowed

to bring a sandwich for lunch.

Or carry a backpack.

Or walk to school.

"Tallulah, you have everything a little girl could ever want, and that's what makes you different," said her father.

Tallulah didn't want to be different.

At school Tallulah wanted
to build a clay mountain
where tiny people could live.

Or draw a purple moose
jumping through a circus hoop.

Or crawl into a
pretend rocket ship and
fly to outer space.

"You'll get dirty."

"You'll ruin your dress."

"You don't fit in," said her classmates.

When lunchtime came, one of the boys in the cafeteria spilled his milk on purpose.

A girl dumped her potato chips on someone's head.

But when Tallulah started to throw
her smoked salmon sushi roll,
the teacher stopped her.

"I'm surprised at you. Girls like
you don't throw food," said the teacher.

Outside on the playground things

got worse.

"You can't climb trees with us."

"You can't dig for treasure with us."

"Look at your big sash. You look like a fancy, gift-wrapped box. No one wants to play with a box!"

"Why not? Don't you guys like presents?"

Tallulah turned to see who was talking.

It was the new boy in school, Max.

"Thank you for sticking up for me," Tallulah said.

"I know what it's like to feel a little bit differ—" Max

stopped in the middle of his sentence. There was a

commotion around the fishpond.

They ran over to see what was going on.

Tallulah saw a tiny, wet puppy floating on a log.

It looked stuck and scared.

"We have to help it!" said Tallulah.

"We can't go in there. The fishpond is disgusting," said one of the kids.

"It's an ugly puppy anyway," said another.

"It looks like a rat," said somebody else.

All the kids ran off except Tallulah and Max.

"I don't think it can swim," said Max.

"Neither can I," said Tallulah.

Then she had an idea. She reached to her sash and pulled—and the big, hideous bow came undone.

Tallulah threw one end of the sash as hard as she could.

It landed right next to the puppy.

The puppy grabbed the ribbon in its teeth.

Tallulah pulled—

her perfect hair got messed up.

And pulled—

her dressy shoes got soaking wet.

And pulled—

mud splashed on
her fancy dress.

"You're a big mess!" said Max, but he was smiling.

"That's the kind of girl I *really* am," said Tallulah, and she pulled that puppy right up onto dry land.

Tallulah dried

the puppy off.

And named her Mimi.

And brought her home.

At home nobody was happy to see the little pug puppy.

"Dogs are dirty!" said her mother.

"Dogs smell

bad," said her father.

"Dogs are messy," said the housekeeper.

Tallulah took a deep breath. She had something to say.

She waited until everyone was looking at her.

"At home everybody tells me I can't do things

because of who I am."

"At school everybody tells me I can't play with them because of who I am. But this is who I *really* am. I like to wear jeans and build clay mountains and rescue dogs, even if they're funny-looking."

"So, please, can I keep Mimi?"

And so the puppy stayed.

Mimi was dirty . . .

but Tallulah cleaned up after her.

Mimi was stinky . . .

but Tallulah always

bathed her.

And sometimes Tallulah

got dirty and stinky and messy herself.

And sometimes everybody needed

an extra bath.

They may have been a little bit
different. But Tallulah and Max and Mimi
were happy just the way they were.